THE BATTLEFIELD
OF LOVE

Jeremy D. Brackett

TABLE OF CONTENTS

OVERVIEW OF THE WORKBOOK

This workbook is specifically designed for newly married couples, or "newlyweds," but married couples at any stage can benefit and find great value from the content provided in this workbook. There are 52 date night activities within this workbook, for every week of the year.

Some activities require feedback to be recorded directly on the page, and other activities allow for social media engagement so others can see how exciting marriage can be. Additionally, there are helpful tips that will be included throughout the workbook that can provide additional insight on maintaining a positive and lasting marriage. Lastly, a married couple of 38 years was interviewed and provided great marital advice that can be reviewed in the frequently asked questions portion of this workbook.

The 52 date night activities found in this workbook are the suggested activities that my wife and I enjoyed on our date nights. It was an opportunity for us to:

1) Learn more about the other.

2) Enjoy activities together as a couple.

3) Truly understand what it takes to combine our lives together as one.

Marriage takes work and is not always easy, but I can honestly say these activities were effective for us. Give it a chance and get back to the basics of learning your spouse all over again. After 13 activities, there will be an opportunity for a mission report to summarize your thoughts of the activities. Remember, love is a battlefield. Are you ready for the challenge soldiers? I believe in you. You have your orders... and you are now dismissed!

ACTIVITY 1
GETTING TO KNOW YOUR PARTNER

Objective: You have already passed the stage of getting to know your partner in dating season. Now you are in unfamiliar territory, marriage. It's now time to get to know your spouse on a deeper level. The goal of this activity is to ask each other questions to facilitate conversations and learn more about your partner. This requires going deeper than the surface. Each person must answer all questions.

Questions:
<u>Childhood:</u>

1. What was the first vacation you remember as a child?

2. What was your favorite food growing up?

3. What is your fondest memory from childhood?

4. What is your earliest happy memory?

5. What is your earliest sad memory?

6. What is something that you wish your family did more of when you were a child?

7. What is something that you wish your family did less of when you were a child?

8. What was something you were insecure about as a child?

9. Name a time when you broke the rules, and were never caught?

10. Who was your first childhood crush?

Goals:

1. What is your proudest accomplishment thus far in life?

2. Where do you see yourself in the next 3 years?

3. Where do you see yourself in the next 5 years?

4. What is the goal that you are currently working toward?

5. Where does your inspiration come from?

6. Who was the last person that you motivated and inspired to pursue something and when?

7. What is your favorite motivational quote?

8. Which celebrity most inspires you?

9. Which one of your family members inspires you most?

10. What was the last goal you obtained?

Relationship:

1. How long have we known each other?

2. What do you like most about our relationship?

3. If you could change one thing about our relationship, what would it be?

4. What is something that I do, that you dislike the most?

5. What have you learned about love and marriage from your family?

6. Do you feel like we do enough fun activities together?

7. Do you feel like we do enough romantic activities together?

8. How often would you like for us to have a date night?

9. Do you feel comfortable enough to cry in front of me?

10. What do you love most about me?

Romance- Intimacy:

1. How do you feel about our intimacy?

2. How do you feel about the amount of intimate moments we share?

3. How many times a week would you like for us to be intimate?

4. What are your favorite sexual positions?

5. What is something that you refuse to do when we make love?

6. How can I better satisfy you sexually?

7. If you had some concerns regarding our intimacy, would you feel comfortable enough to tell me? Why or why not.

8. What are some of your sexual fantasies? (Judgment free zone)

9. Would you be interested in having a "Naked Saturday?"

   Hint: No clothing allowed for the entire day (inside your home).

10. What is your idea of a romantic evening?

Budget:

1. What is your annual salary?

2. How much do you make after paying taxes?

3. Who is a better budgeter? Me, or you?

4. Between the two of us, who would be better at managing our finances?

5. Would you want both of our names on all our bank accounts?

6. What are some of your biggest expenses/ debts?

7. How much would you like to save every pay period?

8. Would you rather save money until you are ready to buy, or use credit and pay for it later?

9. How do you feel about naming accounts specific names based on the purpose they will serve? (Ex: Vacation, Bills, Play, Savings)

10. When it comes to money, are you more of a saver or a spender?

Family:

1. How many children would you like to have?

2. If we were looking for a babysitter in our family, who would you not want to babysit our children?

3. What style of parenting do you have, or will you choose to have when we have children?

4. What are you most nervous about regarding being a parent?

5. How involved do you want to be in our children's life?

6. How do you feel about disciplining our children, and what are the best methods that you would prefer?

7. What are some of the parenting techniques that your parents used, that you want to use in our family?

8. What are some of the parenting techniques that your parents used, that you DO NOT want to use in our family?

9. How do you feel about the way we should resolve conflict in our relationship and family?

10. If our children wanted one of us to keep a secret from the other, would you keep that secret from me? Why or why not?

Personal: Self-awareness:

1. What do you like most about yourself?

2. What is your most attractive feature on your body?

3. What is your favorite sport?

4. What do you like to do for fun?

5. What are your pet peeves?

6. How important is religion to you in our marriage?

7. What are you most embarrassed or self-conscience about?

8. What is something that I say that makes you feel bad?

9. When was the last time I made you laugh?

10. What is your favorite music genre?

Employment:

1. Do you enjoy your job?

2. What are your career aspirations?

3. Is your current job stressful? If so, how do you manage this stress?

4. Would you be willing to relocate for a job?

5. If you were offered a job in a different city, and I was not able to move there right away, would you discuss it with me prior to accepting it?

6. If you were having challenges on your job, would you feel comfortable discussing them with me?

7. If you were no longer interested in your current career, how would you tell me that you wanted to transition to a new career?

8. If you were unhappy with your current job, would you find another job prior to resigning from your current job first?

9. If we needed another source of income for our family, would you be willing to work a 2nd job?

10. How do you feel about doing volunteerism or doing something to help the community?

Random:
1. If we could take a road trip, where would you want to go?

2. If I cleaned one location in our home, what location would most satisfy you?

3. If I gave you a massage, what areas would you want me to focus on?

4. What are your top 5 favorite movies?

5. If we were role playing, what character would you want me to be?

6. What do you think will be the most challenging aspect of marriage?

7. What are your favorite ice cream flavors?

8. If we went on a double date, who would you want to double date with?

9. If we went on a triple date, who would you want to triple date with?

10. What question had the most surprising response from me?

Random Part 2:

1. How often do you like to exercise?

2. What is your favorite exercise to do in the gym?

3. What is a sensitive topic for you?

4. What is your least favorite color?

5. How often do you like to get your hair cut/ styled?

6. Are you still in contact with any of your exes?

7. What was your worst relationship like?

8. Which city have you always wanted to live in, but never could?

9. Would you like it if you had a twin sibling?

10. If you found out that you had a long lost sibling, what would your response be?

Random:

1. How often do you like to exercise?

2. What is your favorite exercise to do in the gym?

3. What is a sensitive topic for you?

4. What is your least favorite color?

5. How often do you like to get your hair cut/ styled?

6. Are you still in contact with any of your exes?

7. What was your worst relationship like?

8. Which city have you always wanted to live in, but never could?

9. Would you like it if you had a twin sibling?

10. If you found out that you had a long lost sibling, what would your response be?

ACTIVITY 2
NICE STROLL IN THE PARK

Objective: There is nothing more relaxing than a nice stroll in the park, especially while watching the sunset or sunrise. A walk in the park allows for both physical activity and great conversation. Try walking while holding hands to show your spouse that well-deserved affection. Finally, wait for the perfect opportunity to capture the moment via a picture and post on social media with the hashtag "BattlefieldofLoveParkLife2."

ACTIVITY 3
GAME NIGHT WITH FRIENDS

Objective: In this activity you and your spouse will have the opportunity to enjoy a little camaraderie. It is game night, and it is time to tag in your friends. There are several games that you and your friends or family can enjoy. One recommended game is Taboo.

It is recommended to play guys against the girls if the numbers are even. If not, discuss how to best divide the teams, with you and your spouse on separate teams. Who will come out on top? Whoever the "winning spouse" is tonight, you can choose any non-monetary prize of your choice. It makes it more competitive when the prize is something romantic and desirable!

Game Night!!!

ACTIVITY 4
MEETING WITH YOUR PERSONAL FINANCIAL ADVISOR- *"YOUR SPOUSE"*

Objective: Finances can be a critical component to ensuring the success of a marriage. It is not necessarily important "how much" your household income is, but what matters most is understanding how the finances will be managed. Issues can arise if one spouse is a "saver", and the other spouse is a "spender."

The goal of this activity is to communicate expectations regarding how finances will be managed, and to develop your first marital budget plan as a couple. Remember, you are about to go to a business meeting so dress to impress. After you and your spouse have completed your meeting with your financial advisor, post a picture of the two of you on social media, with the hashtag "BattlefieldofLoveLifeGoals4."

The Family Budget: (Use a separate document to provide responses to ensure privacy of information and save the document. It is recommended to use a spreadsheet if available.)

A. How many total bills do you currently have?

B. What financial goals do you want to reach in the next 3 months?

C. Discuss potentially having the following bank accounts:
   Note- Lower Priority: #1 and #2, Higher Priority: #3 and #4

   1. Play- What to allot yourselves every pay period to have fun

2. Vacation- What to set aside for when you are ready to travel

3. Goal Oriented Savings: Large items that you plan to buy

4. Emergency Savings: Saving for a rainy day or an emergency

D. What bank/ banks are you affiliated with?

In the Family Budget table: 1) Add partner names, 2) Name of bills with amounts, 3) how much will be allocated in each category. If there are less than 8 bills, then those entries may be left blank.

Family Budget	
Name:	Name:
Monthly Income:	Monthly Income:
Bill 1: Amount:	Bill 1: Amount:
Bill 2: Amount:	Bill 2: Amount:
Bill 3: Amount:	Bill 3: Amount:
Bill 4: Amount:	Bill 4: Amount:
Bill 5: Amount:	Bill 5: Amount:
Bill 6: Amount:	Bill 6: Amount:
Bill 7: Amount:	Bill 7: Amount:
Bill 8: Amount:	Bill 8: Amount:

Total Expenses: Add Bills 1- 8 Ex: Rent, mortgage, car payment, music subscriptions	Total Expenses: Add Bills 1- 8 Ex: Insurance, monthly gas, utility bill, student loan
Total Amount Available: (Income - Expenses)	Total Amount Available: (Income- Expenses)
Play:	Play:
Vacation:	Vacation:
Goal Oriented Savings:	Goal Oriented Savings:
Emergency Savings	Emergency Savings

ACTIVITY 5
LET YOUR TASTE BUDS DO THE TALKING

Objective: In this activity you and your spouse will have the opportunity to enjoy each other's presence while enjoying a romantic snack, chocolate covered strawberries. First, you will need strawberries and chocolate. It is recommended to either use Nestle Toll House Milk Chocolate Morsels, Hershey Milk Chocolate Baking Chips, Ghirardelli baking chips, or Baker's Baking Chocolate bars. Second, you and your spouse will work together to prepare the chocolate covered strawberries. See instructions below:

1. Wash thoroughly and dry the strawberries.

2. Safely melt the chocolate in the microwave and stir every 25 secs (*preference for source used to melt chocolate may vary*).

3. Safely Dip strawberries in the chocolate to coat (*use caution*)

4. Place on a cooking sheet or aluminum foil to allow chocolate to settle (optional).

5. Pick your desired beverage to enjoy with your romantic snack.

Note, the chocolate is optional. The goal is to set a romantic atmosphere, with preferred music and enjoy the "edible" foreplay. Tonight, it is not about winning or losing, but it is about satisfying your spouse's taste buds. Enjoy!

ACTIVITY 6
EXOTIC DESSERT NIGHT

Objective: In this activity you and your spouse will be challenged to work together to create a prodigious (extradentary), edible masterpiece and allow your palates to experience such a beautiful and exotic dessert. It is time to transport your taste buds to paradise. The objective of this activity is to work together to first determine which exotic dessert you and your spouse would like to create. Whether it is something that you found on Pinterest, or something that you found on the Food Network. It is important that you both find it tasteful and fits into your definition of an "exotic dessert."

Remember, be sure to take some pictures to capture your work of art before diving into your Instagram-worthy treat! Once you capture your work of art, post it on social media with the hashtag "BattlefieldofLoveEdibleDelight6" to see if you receive >50 likes (together). If you do, then you both win the activity. Note, if you do not have social media, message 10 friends/ family members with a picture of your dessert, and include hashtag "**BattlefieldofLoveEddibleDelight6**", to see if you receive a thumbs up or thumbs down for your dessert. If you receive a thumbs up from 9 out of 10 friends, you both win the challenge. Note, the goal is to bake an exotic dessert together, but it is up to you if you decide to share it with others, or eat it together. Good luck!

ACTIVITY 7
COMEDY NIGHT: LAUGH OUT LOUD

Objective: In this activity you will have the opportunity to step outside of your home and laugh at your local comedian. Locate the nearest comedy show in your area and get two tickets for you and your spouse. Enjoy a good laugh either with the comedian or at the comedian. After the comedy show, return home and talk about it.

Note, if you are not located near a comedy club, then you can have a comedy night in the comfort of your home. Watch a comedy special online or on a streaming application such as Netflix or Hulu.

Need talking Points: Answer the following questions (*Optional*)

1. What was your favorite joke?

2. What was your least favorite joke?

3. Would you want to see the comedian again?

ACTIVITY 8
INDOOR CAMPING: BRING OUT THE S'MORES

Objective: In this activity you will enjoy a nice, relaxing night inside your home with your spouse. Lay out a blanket on the floor and remember to bring the marshmallows, graham crackers, and Hershey's milk chocolate. Feel free to melt the chocolate and marshmallows to really create the atmosphere.

It's time to use your imagination and describe where you and your spouse have traveled and describe your surroundings. Imagine you are camping out in Bright Angel Campground of the Grand Canyon, or in Miyajima, Japan which is known as "Island of the gods". It is recommended to bring decorations that can really get you in the mindset of camping out. Once you and your spouse have set the decorations, capture your in-home camp site, and post it on social media with the hashtag "BattlefieldofLoveCampOut8." Remember to complete the information below:

Location Traveled: _____ *(Imaginary)*

Describe Scenery Below:

_____

_____

_____

_____

ACTIVITY 9
SPORTS ARENA:
TAKE ME OUT TO THE BALL GAME

Objective: In this activity you and your spouse will choose a sport where you both have a shared interest. It does not matter the level of talent. Feel free to enjoy a high school, college, or a professional sports game. Once you have agreed on the sport, identify a game, and purchase your two tickets. When you arrive to the sporting event, be sure to capture your excitement and post it to social media with the hashtag, "BattlefieldofLoveGameTime9." Remember one of the perks of being there and cheering on your favorite team, are the concessions. Don't forget to enjoy the snacks!

Note, if there are no local sports playing in your area, feel free to enjoy a game in the comfort of your home. Watch a game on television from the beginning to the end.

ACTIVITY 10
DOUBLE DATE NIGHT: TAG YOUR FRIENDS

Objective: In this activity you and your spouse will enjoy the company of two of your friends or family members (one couple). It is completely up to you if you would like to invite your friends/ family over to your home, or out on the town. The decision rests with you.

It is important to remember that no matter the stage of marriage that you are in, whether you are newlyweds or seasoned veterans, it is perfectly fine to enjoy the company of others. At the completion of the evening, capture a picture with your group and post it on social media with the hashtag "BattlefieldofLoveDoubleDateNight10."

What did you like most about hanging out with your friends/ family tonight?

(Record information below after you have returned home):

_____

_____

_____

_____

_____

_____

ACTIVITY 11
BLIND DATE WITH A STRANGER: WHERE ARE YOU FROM?

Objective: It is time for you and your spouse to use your imaginations when it comes to who you are and where you are from. Neither of you are from the local area, and you both are on a blind date that your best friend coordinated. In this activity you and your spouse will role play as if you are completely different people, with new names, on a blind date. Remember since this is a blind date, your best friend has already shared specific characteristics about your spouse that you can share with them. These characteristics are how you see your spouse. Everything you share should come from the heart.

Enjoy a night out on the town with your spouse as complete strangers. Are you talented enough to win your spouse's heart all over again? We shall see. At the completion of the evening, answer the questions below. Good luck!

Answer the following questions and discuss:

1. Where are you both from?

2. What were your names?

3. Were either of you honestly convincing?

ACTIVITY 12
ICE CREAM CREATION: BANANA SPLIT NIGHT

Objective: In this activity you and your spouse will have the opportunity to really enjoy your favorite ice cream dessert with toppings. How creative are you when it comes to creating an edible work of art, in the form of a banana split? Prior to beginning your creation, make a list of all the items that you both will include in your banana split. Remember, you both are a team, which means that you both must agree on all the toppings prior to using them on the banana split. If one spouse does not like the taste of a topping, it cannot be used. This activity will help you both work together as a team and practice your ability to compromise.

Toppings:

1. _____

2. _____

3. _____

4. _____

5. _____

6. _____

7. _____

8. _____

ACTIVITY 13
ROLE PLAY: PASSION VS PLEASURE

Objective: In this activity you and your spouse will have the opportunity to spice things up. First, before you begin the excitement, you and your spouse must first have a conversation about boundaries, soft limits, hard limits, and a safe word. This communication is critical to ensure that neither one of you makes the other uncomfortable in any way. It is important that even though you are role playing, you are still respectful of your spouse and their boundaries.

Role playing is an act of foreplay. It is a great activity to connect with your spouse on a new or unique level romantically. The idea is to use your imagination and create an intimate scene or engage in a fantasy that  you've always dreamed of but never had the courage to bring up. Is someone making a late-night delivery? Is someone staying late after class in their professor's office? Is someone finally meeting that celebrity crush that they always fantasized about? Remember, use your imagination, and see how erotic you two can be.

OBJECTIVE COMPLETE: MISSION REPORT #1

You and your spouse have now completed the **first 13 activities.** Discuss the activities and record your thoughts and feelings about the activities. Which activities do you feel were a one-time-only experience and which do you anticipate repeating with your spouse? Record information below:

_____

_____

_____

_____

_____

_____

_____

_____

_____

_____

_____

_____

_____

_____

_____

_____

HELPFUL TIP #1:
COMPONENTS OF A HEALTHY RELATIONSHIP

Finding "the one," or one's soul mate, can sometimes be difficult. Some people are considered lucky because they find love and their soul mate early in life. While others' discovery of love may be delayed. Regardless of when love is found, the benefits of love will remain the same. Which includes, happiness, excitement, and satisfaction.

Once someone has located their soul mate, then the real work begins. It is not enough to just find one's soul mate, but there must be a commitment to continue cultivating the relationship. There are three primary components that my wife and I have found to be required in our relationship: 1) consistent communication, 2) effective collaboration, and 3) willingness to compromise. These three components, or "The 3 C's," are required to successfully overcome relationship obstacles and emotional battles.

Remember, we said love was beautiful, but we did not say it was easy.

Love can be considered a battlefield because there could be several emotional battles that are presented during the relationship. These emotional battles can sometimes cause couples to individually retreat. This emotional retreat leads to individuals "shutting down" and not conveying their true feelings with the other. These emotional battles can then lead to individuals falling into emotional trenches, where they are so guarded that they are no longer able to work together or collaborate as a team. If couples are unable to make it through these obstacles mentioned above, it could be detrimental to the relationship. Unfortunately, just like in war, relationships can also have casualties, that lead to separation or divorce.

Having the required armor, or in this case the right skills (The 3 C's) needed for a successful relationship and marriage, also means being equipped with the necessary tools to love and enjoy your spouse. Remember the concept that laughter is good for the soul. Having fun with your spouse will bring a closer connection and help you to love each other "to the moon and back," eternally.

Love has always been known to be a beautiful thing. It is like a seed that requires cultivation, time, and attention. It requires the willingness and vulnerability to give away your heart, and the ability to trust that it will not get broken. It requires the openness of one's inner soul, because in those depths is where one's inner self lies. Finally, it requires the awareness that your soul mate will be the person who best compliments you.

ACTIVITY 14
VOLUNTEER DAY: LEND A HELPING HAND

Objective: In this activity you and your spouse will not just put each other first, but it is time to put your community first and lend a helping hand. Brainstorm ideas early in the week, so when date night arrives, you and your spouse can do something that will benefit others. Volunteerism is so rewarding and really helps to bring out your compassionate side.

Having the opportunity to see and enjoy each other's company while helping or serving others is a beautiful experience. When the moment is right, capture a picture of you and your spouse serving the community and post it on social media with the hashtag "BattlefieldofLoveVolunteerDay14." After your activity, remember to complete the entries below:

Volunteer Day (Date): _ _ _ _ _ _ _ _ _ _ _ _ _

Volunteer Location: _ _ _ _ _ _ _ _ _ _ _ _ _

Volunteer Hours: _ _ _ _ _ _ _ _ _ _ _ _

Examples: Habitat for humanity, local food drive, church clean up, feeding at the local shelter, charity events, health fare screenings, or providing support at the local boys and girls club.

ACTIVITY 15
FANTASY ISLAND: WHERE DREAMS COME TRUE

Objective: In this activity you and your spouse have just stumbled across a magic lamp. This magic lamp allows you both to receive four wishes from the other. You will have the opportunity to enjoy something that you've always wanted or previously asked for that does not have a monetary value and cannot be purchased. However, there is a catch: Only one wish can be denied. Choose wisely.

Since you and your spouse will receive four wishes, ensure they are written down on a list, and place the list in a secret location in your home. Now you must give your spouse 3 specific clues to help locate your list, without saying exactly where it is. Once both lists have been located, look over it to identify which wish will be rejected. You can make your lists as innocent as washing dishes, or as promiscuous as you so desire. What happens on Fantasy Island, stays on Fantasy Island. Have fun!

ACTIVITY 16
PROFESSIONAL CHEFS: COUPLES WHO COOK TOGETHER STAY TOGETHER

Objective: In this activity you and your spouse will be able to enjoy a delicious meal, in the comfort of your own home. The best part about it, you and your spouse will be the executive chefs in the kitchen. However, there is a twist. The activity is that the two of you will identify what will be on the menu together. Then, once the menu is finalized, for each dish, one spouse will provide the seasonings and spices for the dish, and the other spouse will choose how it is cooked. Remember you two can work together and talk through anything as needed.

This activity is designed to represent how the two of you must work together as a team, and show how you cannot be successful without the other. Remember, well- seasoned chicken breasts cannot be enjoyed if they are still raw. Once you and your spouse have completed cooking your dinner, capture your cooking skills and post it on social media with the hashtag "BattlefieldofLoveTagTeamChefNight16."

ACTIVITY 17
MEETING WITH YOUR PERSONAL FINANCIAL ADVISOR PART II- *"Your Spouse"*

Objective: Finances can be a critical component to ensuring the success of a marriage. It is not necessarily important "how much" your household income is, but what matters most is understanding how the finances will be managed. Issues can arise if one spouse is a "saver", and the other spouse is a "spender". The goal of this activity is to communicate expectations regarding how finances will be managed, and to develop your second marital budget plan as a couple (Refer to activity 4 for specifics on how to complete the table). Remember, you are about to go to a business meeting so dress to impress. After you and your spouse have completed your meeting with your financial advisor, post on social media, hashtag "BattleofLoveLifeGoals17."

The Family Budget:

1. How many total bills do you currently have?

2. Did you meet your 3-month financial goal? (Refer to activity 4)

3. What financial goals do you want to reach in the next 3 months?

Family Budget	
Name:	Name:
Monthly Income:	Monthly Income:

Bill 1: Amount:	Bill 1: Amount:
Bill 2: Amount:	Bill 2: Amount:
Bill 3: Amount:	Bill 3: Amount:
Bill 4: Amount:	Bill 4: Amount:
Bill 5: Amount:	Bill 5: Amount:
Bill 6: Amount:	Bill 6: Amount:
Bill 7: Amount:	Bill 7: Amount:
Bill 8: Amount:	Bill 8: Amount:
Total Expenses: Add Bills 1- 8 Ex: Rent, mortgage, car payment, music subscriptions	Total Expenses: Add Bills 1- 8 Ex: Insurance, monthly gas, utility bill, student loan
Total Amount Available: (Income- Expenses)	Total Amount Available: (Income- Expenses)
Play:	Play:
Vacation:	Vacation:
Goal Oriented Savings:	Goal Oriented Savings:
Emergency Savings	Emergency Savings

ACTIVITY 18
BINGE WATCH YOUR FAVORITE TV SHOW

Objective: In this activity you and your spouse will have the opportunity to first select a critically acclaimed television show, and binge watch it together. Binge watching a television show together allows for a great opportunity to spend time together. This activity may continue past one night, and that is perfectly fine. It is really satisfying to share a common interest with your spouse and to be able to share your thoughts on the show with your spouse.

Don't forget the popcorn and the chocolate covered raisins! Note, it is recommended to utilize social media to gather some additional input and recommendations from others regarding which show is bingeworthy. Once you have posted the inquiry on social media, remember to add the hashtag **"BattlefieldofLoveBingeNight18."**

ACTIVITY 19
EXPERIENCE AN AMUSEMENT PARK: ENJOY A RUSHING THRILL

Objective: In this activity you and your spouse will agree on an amusement park that you both would like to visit. This activity will allow you to enjoy a rushing thrill by having the opportunity to get on roller coasters and play various games in hopes of winning prizes. Enjoy the food, sun, and excitement as you experience a rush of adrenaline.

Share your thoughts of the amusement Park below:

1. What amusement park did you experience?

2. What did you like most about the amusement park?

3. What did you like the least about the amusement park?

ACTIVITY 20
ESCAPE ROOM: CAN YOU MAKE A GREAT ESCAPE

Objective: In this activity you and your spouse will find a nearby escape room to complete the challenge. An escape room is a local business that allows you to work as a team to find specific codes, secret pathways, and/or clues to resolve a mystery that will allow you to find your way to an escape. It will allow you and your spouse to collaborate as a team. Do you and your spouse have what it takes? We shall see.

Note: If there is no escape room near you, feel free to create one yourself. The idea would be to create hints and clues that will lead to another clue. You can hide your clues throughout your home and have your spouse work through them. Are you clever enough to solve your spouse's riddle?

Escape Room Topic:

Were you and your spouse able to escape?

Share your thoughts with each other regarding the experience:

_____

_____

_____

_____

_____

_____

ACTIVITY 21
CRAFTY LOVE: ARTS AND CRAFTS NIGHT

Objective: In this activity you and your spouse will explore your creative sides. Your mission is to create a masterpiece using a minimum of 3 and a maximum of 5 different items from the list below. You must work together to ensure the required number of items have been used in your shared creation, and that both of you were able to add your creativity to the project.

Gift Basket:

1. Paint brush

2. Paint

3. Construction Paper or Canvas

4. Markers

5. Colored Pencils

6. Crayons

7. Glue or Glitter Glue

8. Other (1 Item of Your Choice): _____

ACTIVITY 22
TAKE OUT AT HOME:
IN THE COMFORT OF YOUR BIRTHDAY SUIT

Objective: In this activity you and your spouse will be able to enjoy dinner (Take out or home cooked meal) and eat it in the comfort of your own home. However, this is not your typical Friday night, "eat in" night. Tonight, you will have the opportunity to enjoy your dinner, with the freedom and opportunity of going commando!

You can not only enjoy the taste of your dinner, but also enjoy the scenery of your spouse. This will be a great opportunity to make the connection that you are not dating anymore, but you have progressed to the next level. Sit back, get comfortable, and enjoy your spouse's birthday suit. Furthermore, it is up to you what you choose to do for dessert.

ACTIVITY 23
THE FORBIDDEN DANCE

Objective: In this activity you and your spouse will have an opportunity to step out of your comfort zone and dance the night away. Have either of you tried the Lambada dance? If not, take some time to do a little research to identify what it is. Some say there is nothing steamier than the art of Lambada, maybe because it is considered, "The forbidden dance."

It is an opportunity to allow you and your spouse to exhibit your masculinity and femininity in dance. It allows you to get close to your spouse and enjoy the sense of closeness and touch. If you have never experienced this forbidden dance, or don't really have a talent for it, it is perfectly fine. Note, if you aren't quite ready to show off your skills in a public place, you can enjoy the Lambada dance in the privacy of your own home. All you need is YouTube, romantic lighting, and you're all set to enjoy dancing the night away. Did I also mention that there will be sweat involved?

ACTIVITY 24
STARGAZING: CAN YOU COUNT THE STARS?

Objective: In this activity you and your spouse will have the opportunity to slow things down a little and have a nice quiet night out under the stars. Whether you choose laying out in your local park, sitting in your car, or even the privacy of your backyard, you and your spouse can just wind down and enjoy the scenery of the midnight skies. How many stars can you count? When you see the stars, what do you think about? Can you locate the milky way? Are you able to identify any planets? Will tonight be the night you see a shooting star?

These are the questions that you should ask your spouse. The goal is not about testing your knowledge of the solar system, but the goal is to bond over an activity that sometimes we do not take advantage of. It may be a good idea to discuss your hopes, dreams, and plans for your future together. Just remember, someone once said, if you shoot for the moon and miss, at least you'll land among the stars.

ACTIVITY 25
EXPRESS YOUR EMOTIONS THROUGH POETRY/ SPOKEN WORD

Objective: "Roses are red, violets are blue, I'm not a true poet but neither are you…" except for tonight! It is time to transform yourself into Emily Dickinson or Langston Hughes. Tonight, you will be developing and sharing your words of truth through spoken word. It can be based on your true feelings or your interests. Remember, all poems don't necessarily need to rhyme, but it does make it sound a little better when it does.

So tonight, turn down the lights, turn on smooth jazz, set the mood right because you never know what talent your spouse has. Take the time and allow your thoughts to flow. Before you know it, you'll sound like a pro. The time has come to write down your words of truth, go ahead and step in the booth. Speak from your heart and express your true feeling. You may soon learn that you find it appealing. After you recite your poem through spoken word, take the time to talk about what you just heard.

ACTIVITY 26
CELEBRATION NIGHT

Congratulations! You have successfully made it halfway through your relationship missions. You have done a wonderful job so far. Every ounce of your effort that you exert into your marriage will have a positive effect in the end. Remember, your marriage will be as good as you make it.

Objective: In this activity you and your spouse will enjoy the opportunity for celebration. Bring out the balloons, candles, cake, and ice cream because it is a celebration. You have worked so hard, and you have made it to this point. In this celebration, you can enjoy any activity that your heart desires. You are celebrating, so whatever activity you feel would allow you to celebrate this great milestone, go for it. It's important to celebrate the small victories. The activity can also be a repeat of a previous activity.

You and your spouse have now completed activities 14- 26. Discuss the activities and record your thoughts and feelings about the activities. Which activities do you feel were a one-time-only experience and which do you anticipate repeating with your spouse? Record information below:

_____

_____

_____

_____

_____

_____

_____

_____

_____

_____

_____

_____

HELPFUL TIP #2: THE IMPORTANCE OF DATING

One method to help ensure that your flame is never extinguished, is to ensure that you continue with some of the ideas that you used during the time when you were dating, or "Dating Season." For example, when my wife and I married, we maintained the idea of date night on Friday nights. Our goal was to have a date night every Friday night that included either: a creative activity that helped us to learn more about the other, a fun game that allowed us to be competitive and laugh together, or a relaxing and romantic evening alone.

It is extremely important as a married couple that you do not get complacent in the relationship and stop entertaining your spouse. You must continue to do the things that led to your spouse falling in love with you from the beginning. Although marriage may not always go as smoothly as you prefer, remember the harder you work at it the easier it will become. It is your role and responsibility of being a spouse to not accept an excitement free marriage, because at the end of the day, marriage is what you make it.

Marriage should include happiness, laughter, and passion. Remember, your spouse is your forever partner.

ACTIVITY 27
PERSONAL SATISFACTION: *"Me Time"*

Objective: In this activity you and your spouse will have the opportunity to enjoy a little "Me Time". Yes, you heard that correctly. For tonight's activity, you and your spouse will first discuss what activity you would really like to do independently, plan it, and then do it separately. Whether it is catching the latest action movie that came out in the movie theater, going to the nearest diner and ordering breakfast for dinner, or just spending time alone in "the man cave". The idea of tonight is to remember that you two have an amazing relationship, and you are a team, but also remember that it is perfectly fine to spend some time alone or away from your spouse.

Remember, just like other activities, you and your spouse must discuss boundaries. Whether those boundaries include not seeing a movie because you both would like to see it together, not going to the new restaurant that just opened downtown because you both wanted to experience it together, or even what time you both are planning to return home. That is a discussion that you and your spouse must have. At the end of the evening, it is important to return home and discuss your activities with one another. Discuss what you enjoyed most, and what you didn't like. Everyone needs a little personal satisfaction via "Me Time."

ACTIVITY 28
KARAOKE NIGHT: SONGS FOR THE DECADES

Objective: Time to step outside of your comfort zone and utilize those vocals! Let's take it back to when music just made you feel good inside. Go back through time and find those old school music artists and sing along. Then, as you go through some of the old school material, transition through the decades from the 60's, 70's, 80's, 90's and early 2000's. Then try some of the newly released songs. Music is good for the soul, no matter the genre. Enjoy a karaoke night with your spouse. Sing, laugh, and dance the night away. You can enjoy karaoke night in the comfort of your own home.

(**Note**: *YouTube is a great source to find songs eligible for karaoke*)

ACTIVITY 29
BOWLING NIGHT:
KEEP YOUR BALLS OUT OF THE GUTTER

Objective: In this activity you and your spouse will have the opportunity to get a little competitive and enjoy bowling together. Bowling is a great activity to have fun and compete. Remember, you don't have to be a professional bowler to have fun. So, if neither one of you are great bowlers, it will provide an opportunity for great laughs. I know you are used to getting hot and steamy with your spouse, but tonight, your night can start off with this fun activity. Just because you are bowling it does not mean that you cannot be flirtatious with your spouse. Just remember, try to keep your balls out of the gutter, no pun intended. Note, several bowling alleys offer various specials based on the day and time that you go. Check local listings to find the best financial discounts.

ACTIVITY 30
MEETING WITH YOUR PERSONAL FINANCIAL ADVISOR PART III- "YOUR SPOUSE"

Objective: Finances can be a critical component to ensuring the success of a marriage. It is not necessarily important "how much" your household income is, but what matters most is understanding how the finances will be managed. Issues can arise if one spouse is a "saver", and the other spouse is a "spender". The goal of this activity is to communicate expectations regarding how finances will be managed, and to develop your third marital budget plan as a couple (Refer to activity 4 for specifics on how to complete the table). Remember, you are about to go to a business meeting so dress to impress.

The Family Budget:

1. How many total bills do you currently have?

2. Did you meet your 3-month financial goal? (Refer to activity 17)

3. What financial goals do you want to reach in the next 3 months?

Family Budget	
Name:	Name:
Monthly Income:	Monthly Income:
Bill 1: Amount:	Bill 1: Amount:
Bill 2: Amount:	Bill 2: Amount:
Bill 3: Amount:	Bill 3: Amount:
Bill 4: Amount:	Bill 4: Amount:
Bill 5: Amount:	Bill 5: Amount:
Bill 6: Amount:	Bill 6: Amount:
Bill 7: Amount:	Bill 7: Amount:
Bill 8: Amount:	Bill 8: Amount:
Total Expenses: Add Bills 1- 8 Ex: Rent, mortgage, car payment, music subscriptions	Total Expenses: Add Bills 1- 8 Ex: Insurance, monthly gas, utility bill, student loan
Total Amount Available: (Income - Expenses)	Total Amount Available: (Income- Expenses)
Play:	Play:

Vacation:	Vacation:
Goal Oriented Savings:	Goal Oriented Savings:
Emergency Savings	Emergency Savings

ACTIVITY 31
WOULD YOU RATHER: THE QUESTIONNAIRE

Objective: In this activity you and your spouse will continue to get to know each other a little better. You have enjoyed 30 activities thus far and some of them may have allowed you to see a different side of your spouse that you weren't familiar with. That is perfectly fine. Marriage is about learning and growing together. Your interests today may not be the same interests that you had a month ago or that you'll have next year. Your interest changes with your experiences. Listed below are several "would you rather" questions to get the conversation started. Add 13 additional "would you rather" questions that you are truly interested in learning about your spouse, to turn it into 21 questions.

Would You Rather:

1. Go to the movies or go out to eat?

2. Make love in the bedroom or another location?

3. Cook dinner or wash the dishes?

4. Rent an apartment or buy a house?

5. Lease a car or buy a car?

6. Take a road trip in a car, bus, train, or airplane?

7. Stay at a family members house on vacation or get a hotel?

8. Use condoms or birth control?

ACTIVITY 32
READ A BOOK TOGETHER: EXPAND YOUR MIND

Objective: In this activity you and your spouse will enjoy the opportunity of reading a book together. Reading is a great way to expand your mind. It doesn't matter if you like to read the autobiography of Thomas Jefferson, or the latest James Patterson novel, but what matters most is that you two are able to compromise on a book that both of you find interesting and can enjoy. It is relaxing being cuddled up with your spouse and rotating reading to one another. It brings satisfaction just knowing that you are doing something different than the norm on a date night with your spouse.

ACTIVITY 33
GAME NIGHT: BATTLE OF THE SEXES

Objective: In this activity you and your spouse will have the opportunity to enjoy game night! You and your spouse can select your favorite game from childhood, high school, college, or any game that you love to play. Let's bring the "inner child" out of you two tonight. Game night is a great opportunity to laugh and have fun with your spouse. Who doesn't enjoy a little taunting and allowing their competitive juices to flow? Ordinarily you're a team, but tonight it is everyone for themselves. Game night is specifically for you and your spouse only. It is battle of the sexes. See who will come out on top tonight, no pun intended?

Name of Game: _____

Game Night Winner: _____

Game Night Prize: _____

Congratulations!!!!!

ACTIVITY 34
WHAT ARE YOUR FEARS: I'LL BE YOUR HERO

Objective: In this activity you and your spouse will have the opportunity to sit back, drink some hot chocolate or hot tea while you discuss your biggest fears. The purpose of this activity is to relax, get comfortable, and be vulnerable with each other. When you think of love, it is giving your heart to someone and trusting that they won't break it. Being vulnerable with your spouse is a great way to learn the most intricate details about what is really in their heart.

Having a conversation about your fears is a method to "open up" about what really scares you. There is no better person to have this conversation with than the person who vowed to love you. No matter what, they promised to be there with you and for you. When you and your spouse discuss your fears, be sure to listen attentively and be mindful not to be judgmental. Your only job is to listen and remind them that no matter what, you will always be their hero. You just have an invisible cape.

ACTIVITY 35
BRAINSTORM A BUSINESS IDEA:
WHO'S YOUR BOSS

Objective: In this activity you and your spouse will have the opportunity to create a business plan and enjoy the planning phases. It is time to expose your inner entrepreneurial mindset. Discuss with your spouse a potential business idea. It doesn't matter if the business idea is feasible currently or in the future, but the goal is to show that you can dream big. Who knows your idea may just be the next Bitcoin or Facebook idea?

It is important to consider the following:

1. Which industry you have an interest in.

2. A potential need that you and your spouse could provide.

3. A potential issue that you and your spouse could solve.

4. Your business name.

5. Potential startup cost.

6. The potential logistics that would be needed for start-up.

Once you have considered the 6 important steps above, it is now time to develop your business plan with as much specific information as possible. Lastly, remember this is a business meeting with your spouse, so be sure to dress professionally.

ACTIVITY 36
TAKE A BATH TOGETHER

Objective: In this activity you and your spouse will have the opportunity to enjoy a sensual moment tonight in a nice, steamy shower or bubble bath. Feel free to add the rose pedals, light the candles, and/ or play music. Taking a bath isn't about the act of cleaning the body, but it is about enjoying the closeness of your spouse. Use this opportunity to talk about your day, and anything else on your mind. Remember to enjoy this sensual moment, because afterwards, it may lead into something a little steamier.

ACTIVITY 37
EXERCISE NIGHT:
"SWEAT TOGETHER STAY TOGETHER"

Objective: In this activity, you and your spouse will have the opportunity to get your heart pumping and sweat glands functioning. It's time to exercise together. Are you a long-distance runner or a sprinter? Do you like to work on your upper body or lower body? Do you like strengthening your core? Well, it's time to work toward strengthening the core of your relationship by being each other's personal wellness coach.

Encourage the other to do one more push up, or one more sit up. Exercising together really promotes a healthy lifestyle. You are showing your spouse that you don't mind exerting the extra effort, hard work, and/ or dedication to keep your body in optimal shape. Remember you may need to compromise on some of the activities or exercises that you choose, but the overall goal is to break a sweat!

ACTIVITY 38
VOLUNTEER DAY: LEND A HELPING HAND

Objective: In this activity you and your spouse will not just put each other first, but it is time to put your community first and lend a helping hand for a 2nd time. This is a repeat activity because it really emphasizes the importance of helping others. Brainstorm ideas with your spouse early in the week, so when date night arrives, you and your spouse can do something that will benefit others. Volunteerism is so rewarding and really helps you feel like a compassionate individual. Having the opportunity to see and enjoy each other's company while helping or serving others is a beautiful experience. After your activity, remember to complete the entries below:

Volunteer Day (Date): _____

Volunteer Location: _____

Volunteer Hours: _____

ACTIVITY 39
HELLO STRANGER: NICE TO MEET YOU

Objective: In this activity you and your spouse will have the opportunity to get out of the house and go on a date with someone you have never met. Yes, you heard that correctly. You and your spouse will go on a date with someone you have never met, figuratively speaking only. It is time to enjoy a little role playing with your spouse in public.

You and your spouse are to choose completely different identities and meet up at public location where one of you will approach the other and spark a conversation. It is your job to impress your spouse and enjoy a first date with your spouse. Do you have enough charm and charisma to have a lovely first date with your spouse? If the first date goes well, who knows, you may be able to get your spouse back to your place for a little extracurricular activity. Also, a name tag is optional.

Note, this activity is similar to Activity 11. However, the primary difference is in this activity you do not know anything about your spouse. This means that you must share with your spouse who you really are and what you think of yourself. Remember self-confidence is the best confidence. Good luck.

OBJECTIVE COMPLETE: MISSION REPORT #3

You and your spouse have now completed activities 27- 39. Discuss the activities and record your thoughts and feelings about the activities. Which activities do you feel were a one-time-only experience and which do you anticipate repeating with your spouse? Record information below:

_____

_____

_____

_____

_____

_____

_____

_____

_____

_____

_____

_____

_____

_____

_____

_____

HELPFUL TIP #3: MANAGING DISAGREEMENTS

Many people believe disagreements in a marriage portrays an undesirable relationship. I prefer to believe that disagreements are absolutely expected. Disagreements are normal and can be helpful to the relationship when it is conducted in an appropriate manner. Everyone has a different form of communication. However, to have a disagreement and successfully move pass that disagreement requires four specific rules to be maintained and followed: 1) Contemplate what you plan to say, prior to saying it, 2) Never belittle your partner, 3) Maintain your composure, and 4) Be willing to compromise.

Contemplating what you plan to say is extremely important because once words are communicated, they cannot be retracted. When couples are in heated discussions, they tend to say the first thing that comes to mind. These words are most likely being said out of anger. In this state of anger, these words can also lead to someone belittling their partner or fighting below the belt.

Fighting below the belt can be detrimental to the relationship. Fighting below the belt negatively impacts the other individual's self-confidence. Our goal as a spouse should never be to tear down our partner, but to build them up.

The true definition of "partner" means that you are on the same team and that you should be working toward the same common goal.

It is also crucial to have the ability to maintain composure. Maintaining composure means to have self-control. If you need a moment away from your spouse to regroup, that is acceptable. The key factor to remember is to communicate that intent. Your spouse should not see you walk away with no communication, because it gives the misconception that you are running away from the disagreement and quitting on your partner.

Lastly, one key factor to remember, that has been discussed before is being willing to compromise. Remember just because you are married does not mean that you will always agree on everything. You are two different individuals, with different ideas, beliefs, and histories. You should not expect to always convince your spouse to agree with your frame of thinking on every topic. Everyone is entitled to their own opinion. Furthermore, just like there are topics that you do not always have to agree on, be mindful that there are other important topics that you two must be able to come to an agreement on or a compromise. For example, making big purchases such as buying a new home, or making major life decisions such as planning to have children requires a mutual consensus.

In summary, disagreements are normal and can be helpful to the relationship when it is conducted in an appropriate manner. It can be helpful because it allows your spouse to understand how you feel on specific topics and learn from it. It is true that every relationship is different. Everyone's process of how they disagree will be different. However, I challenge you and your spouse to utilize the key factors that we discussed above in any disagreement that is encountered. In addition, it is important for you both to identify other important factors that you both need to implement during disagreements to ensure you can have them, and then move pass them in a positive manner.

ACTIVITY 40
TREAT ME LIKE ROYALTY:
HOW CAN I SERVE YOU?

Objective: You and your spouse will have the opportunity experience the life of royalty. It is time for one spouse to sit back, relax, and prepare to be served, and the other to provide the service. One spouse is in control and must follow every command for 1 hour. It doesn't matter what the request is, every command must be granted. After the 1 hour is complete, the roles should be switched. The time has come to sit back and allow your spouse to ask you, how can I serve you tonight?

ACTIVITY 41
ROAD TRIP: ENJOY THE OPEN ROAD

Objective: In this activity you and your spouse will have the opportunity to get out and enjoy a road trip. You can extend date night, into a fun and exciting weekend. Taking a road trip with your spouse is a perfect opportunity to just have casual conversation and talk about anything that is on your mind. You don't have to have deep conversations; you just need to have an open dialogue. Of course, there is a twist. In this activity, one spouse is to choose the direction in which to travel, and the other spouse chooses the actual city.

Remember for the one that chooses the direction, it is important to be as specific as possible. Is it northwest, southeast, or it is truly just south? The spouse that chooses the city, should do their best to choose a city that they believe the other spouse will also enjoy. It is up to both of you to plan the logistics. Do you need to book a hotel, or will it be a day trip? Are there any special activities that you both want to do? Are there any friends or family nearby that you would like to visit? On your trip, remember to have fun!

ACTIVITY 42
PAINTING WITH PASSION: THE ART OF LOVE

Objective: Painting can sometimes inspire someone to show more of their "creative side". Spice things up and have a "Sip and Design" night at home. Enjoy a glass of sparkling cider, or a nice fine Muscadine wine (which ever you prefer). The primary goal is to draw and paint whatever makes you happy. Allow your "creative juices" to flow!

Spark a conversation about whatever is on your mind. Remember general small talk with your spouse is perfectly fine. You don't have to have deep emotional conversations every night. The concept is that you and your spouse must understand that it doesn't matter what the topic of conversation is, but what matters most is that communication exists. Kick back and enjoy your "Sip and Design" Night. If you are not artistically gifted, this can also take the form of buying a "Paint by Numbers" picture, and painting with that. The "Paint by Numbers" picture provides an outlined, black, and white picture, with a legend to tell you what color each section should be. Enjoy this "Sip and design" activity because you never know, it may be worth framing.

ACTIVITY 43
MEETING WITH YOUR PERSONAL FINANCIAL ADVISOR PART IV- "YOUR SPOUSE"

Objective: Finances can be a critical component to ensuring the success of a marriage. It is not necessarily important "how much" your household income is, but what matters most is understanding how the finances will be managed. Issues can arise if one spouse is a "saver", and the other spouse is a "spender". The goal of this activity is to communicate expectations regarding how finances will be managed, and to develop your fourth marital budget plan as a couple (Refer to activity 4 for specifics on how to complete the table). Remember, you are about to go to a business meeting so dress to impress.

The Family Budget:

1. How many total bills do you currently have?

2. What will be your next bill that you will completely pay off?

3. Did you meet your 3-month financial goal? (Refer to activity 30)

4. What financial goals do you want to reach in the next 3 months?

Family Budget

Name:	Name:
Monthly Income:	Monthly Income:
Bill 1: Amount:	Bill 1: Amount:
Bill 2: Amount:	Bill 2: Amount:
Bill 3: Amount:	Bill 3: Amount:
Bill 4: Amount:	Bill 4: Amount:
Bill 5: Amount:	Bill 5: Amount:
Bill 6: Amount:	Bill 6: Amount:
Bill 7: Amount:	Bill 7: Amount:
Bill 8: Amount:	Bill 8: Amount:
Total Expenses: Add Bills 1- 8 Ex: Rent, mortgage, car payment, music subscriptions	Total Expenses: Add Bills 1- 8 Ex: Insurance, monthly gas, utility bill, student loan
Total Amount Available: (Income- Expenses)	Total Amount Available: (Income- Expenses)
Play:	Play:
Vacation:	Vacation:
Goal Oriented Savings:	Goal Oriented Savings:

Emergency Savings	Emergency Savings

ACTIVITY 44
IDENTIFY A PROJECT TO WORK ON IN YOUR HOME TOGETHER

Objective: In this activity you and your spouse will have the opportunity to do a little bonding and work on a project together. It doesn't matter if the project is redecorating your bedroom, putting together a bookshelf, or even putting up decorations on a wall. Working on household projects together can be challenging for a couple. It requires patience, understanding, and willingness to make mistakes without getting upset. Sometimes working on projects together can even put your relationship to the test. That is perfectly fine, just remember it is an obstacle that you can make it through. Be sure to utilize each other strengths. At the end of your project, it will be really satisfying to know that you both completed something together as a team. No matter how it looks, you both should still feel accomplished.

ACTIVITY 45
BAKE OFF: WHAT'S YOUR BEST DESSERT?

Objective: In this activity you and your spouse will have the opportunity to enjoy a little competition. It is a dessert bake off. You and your spouse will each make one of your world-famous desserts, and then allow the other to taste. Remember it is important that you answer truthfully. If it is identified to be a tie, you can solicit feedback from friends or family members.

Remember if an outside taster is utilized, ensure your taster is not aware of who baked which dessert to remove any unconscious bias. The taste testing should be completely anonymous. This activity is great because it really allows a spouse to exhibit their talents. Keep in mind, based on the outcome, you'll soon find out who will be responsible for baking desserts for any future family functions.

ACTIVITY 46
MOVIE NIGHT: ALL TIME CLASSICS

Objective: In this activity you and your spouse must first list the top 5 movie classics of all time. Once you both have listed your top 5 favorite movies, compare your lists, and identify any movies that were the same. Whatever movies you both share on your lists, circle them, and then vote on one of the movies that are circled to watch for movie night. If there are no common movies on your lists, then each person should circle the #1 movie on the other person's list and be prepared to watch both!

(**Disclaimer**: Feel free to use Saturday night if you need it.)

ACTIVITY 47
VISIT WITH FAMILY

Objective: In this activity you and your spouse will have the opportunity to go back to your roots and visit family. Although visiting family can seem trivial, having a good relationship with your spouse's family can also lead to a strong foundation of love for you and your spouse. Once you have visited your family, post it to social media, and include hashtag "BattlefieldofLoveFamilyMattersMost47." Remember, home is where the heart is.

Family Matters Most.

ACTIVITY 48
PHOTOSHOOT WITH YOUR SPOUSE

Objective: In this activity you and your spouse will have the opportunity to each stand behind the lens and capture your Kodak moments of each other. You both will be able to show off your modeling skills in a photo-shoot. You can have as many outfit changes as you like and explore various locations to experience a different atmosphere.

It has been stated by several photographers that photography documents your journey as you progress through life. This photoshoot is an excellent opportunity to create memories that will last for a lifetime. It should be full of fun and excitement and allow you to capture the moments that will take your breath away. Once you and your spouse have enjoyed your personal photo- shoot together, ensure you save one picture each, and post it on social media with the hashtag "BattlefieldofLoveMemoriesForALifetime48." Note, you don't need the most expensive camera to show off your style and beauty, as camera phones will do just fine.

ACTIVITY 49
TRIPLE DATE NIGHT: TAG YOUR FRIENDS

Objective: In this activity you and your spouse will enjoy the company of four of your friends/ family (2 sets of couples). It is completely up to you if you would like to invite your group over to your home, or out on the town (ex. Dinner, bowling, movies, etc.). The decision rests with you.

It is important to remember that no matter the stage of marriage that you are in, whether you are newlyweds or seasoned marital veterans, it is encouraged to enjoy the company of others. At the completion of the evening, capture a picture with your group and post it on social media with the hashtag "BattlefieldofLoveTripleDateNight49." At the completion of the evening, ask your friends to print their names below:

Couple 1: _____

Couple 2: _____

What did you like most about hanging out with your friends tonight?

_____

_____

_____

_____

_____

_____

ACTIVITY 50
LET'S BE ADVENTUROUS

Objective: In this activity you and your spouse will have the opportunity to experience an intense adrenaline rush. Experiencing an activity that will really have your heart pumping. An adrenaline filled activity with your spouse can really bring a lot of joy and excitement to the relationship. This activity is not a specific activity, but more so to provide options for you and your spouse. Discuss how much you and your spouse will lean into discomfort.

It has been stated that moments of adrenaline rushes can lead to sexual attraction. Reference recommendations below for possible adventure seeking activities. Note, once you have completed the activity, post a picture on social media, with the hashtag "BattlefieldofLoveAdventurousLove50," of you and your spouse enjoying your exciting activity together. Remember, you want to experience an adrenaline rush so just go for it!

Options:

1. Skydiving/ Indoor Skydiving
2. Go-kart Racing
3. Gun Range
4. Motorcycle Ride

5. Water Skiing/ Surfing
6. Base Jumping
7. Zip Lining
8. Rock Climbing

ACTIVITY 51
BREAKFAST, LUNCH, DINNER:
WHERE-EVER WE GO OUR LOVE WON'T CHANGE

Objective: In this activity you and your spouse will have the opportunity to enjoy breakfast at home or in your home city, lunch >30 miles away from your home, and dinner >60 miles away from your home. Note, choose restaurants that you or your spouse have never experienced, or pack your lunch and dinner to travel with you. This would be a great opportunity to find various parks or outdoor eating areas for your lunch and dinner.

This activity can lead to numerous possibilities and a new adventure. You could enjoy the scenery in the locations that you choose and who knows, there could be some fun activities to do in those areas as well. For each location where you dine, capture a photo of you and your spouse and include the hashtag, "BattlefieldofLoveAdventurousFoodie51". At the end of the evening, you should include 3 different pictures in your post: one from breakfast, lunch, and dinner. Wherever your adventure leads you, even if the scenery changes, your love will remain the same.

ACTIVITY 52
CELEBRATION NIGHT!

Congratulations! You and your spouse have finally reached the last activity of your mission. As we stated before, whenever you complete anything or accomplish a milestone, enjoy a celebration. You must remember to celebrate the small victories and the little wins.

Marriage comes with many challenges that you and your spouse will need to be equipped and prepared to endure. If you both continue to work together as a team and utilize some of the qualities that this workbook has enhanced, you two will be able to make it through anything. Remember, it's not about each person giving 50 % effort (50/ 50), but each person must give 100% of themselves to help ensure that the marriage continues to work.

In your celebration tonight dress to impress. Bring out your best outfits and the best version of your authentic selves and enjoy an evening with your spouse. Remember to light candles, turn on the music, bring some flowers, and open the bubbly, because you and your spouse deserve a wonderful evening of love. Again, congratulations and job well done. Your mission is complete!

OBJECTIVE COMPLETE: MISSION REPORT #4

You and your spouse have now completed activities 40- 52. Discuss the activities and record your thoughts and feelings about the activities. Which activities do you feel were a one-time-only experience and which do you anticipate repeating with your spouse? Record information below:

_____

_____

_____

_____

_____

_____

_____

_____

_____

_____

_____

_____

_____

_____

_____

_____

Trust is required to be a pillar of the relationship. Experiencing a marriage where trust has been developed and maintained allows for each spouse to be completely vulnerable with the other. I believe without trust it is extremely difficult for a happy marriage to last. When both spouses are genuinely honest with the other, it allows for full transparency to exist.

As I previously stated, love requires the willingness to give away your heart, and the ability to trust that it will not get broken. When you are continuously honest, truthful, and trusting with your partner it allows you to continue to understand why you initially made a commitment to them. Marriage is challenging. Sometimes there are situations that can seem to be so difficult that it would lead to a spouse questioning the relationship.

Reflecting to the beginning of this workbook, I mentioned that in marriage you and your spouse may experience emotional battles that can lead to an emotional retreat. These emotional battles could impact the trust factor in the relationship. It is your responsibility as a couple to work through problems by brainstorming solutions. You and your spouse are the captains of your relationship. Whichever direction you steer your relationship, that is the direction that it will go. Remember the activities and ideas that were practiced throughout this workbook. They allowed the opportunity to build strong communication skills, team working skills, and lastly enhanced the ability and willingness to compromise.

Love is a battlefield. Love and marriage isn't about who can defeat the other, but it is about how your love can survive the battle of life. Helping your marriage survive requires building and maintaining trust with your partner. It also requires you both to work together as a team to overcome any challenge or obstacle that may appear. Well done comrades, you have now completed your mission and you are dismissed.

MARITAL ADVICE: FREQUENTLY ASKED QUESTIONS (FAQS)

Love, marriage, and relationships may sometimes seem as if it's a battlefield because it has unfamiliar terrain with unexpected challenges and difficulties. At times, the best way to navigate through it successfully is with guidance. Marriage requires two people to consistently communicate and grow in love, because at the end of the day, your marriage is what you make it.

Dr. Melody Brackett, and Elder George Brackett Sr. have been married for 38 years and counting. When interviewed, they stated that there is no formula for how to make a marriage work, but there are helpful tips and tools that can be utilized to make it a little easier to navigate. To provide some additional insight, they were asked 21 questions that pertains to marriage and relationships. Let's look inside their care package to see if they can help us navigate through this battlefield called love.

The Interview- Frequently Asked Questions (FAQs)

1. What do you think are the top 3 qualities every marriage should have?
    Response: Love, Respect, and Honesty

2. In a marriage, is it important to discuss what your own intimate needs, and intimate preferences are?

    Response: Yes, so your spouse can express their needs to you, and to remove the guess work from the relationship. It is important to express your needs to your spouse to ensure your spouse is comfortable and agree with your form of intimacy. It is important to communicate to ensure both of your needs are met, and because you never know if your spouse has experienced any type of trauma related to any intimate activity in the past.

3. How do you work together and plan financially?

   Response: You must first work together to identify a vision for your family. Then you must work together to set agreed upon mutual goals, and faithfully work toward them. Then once a goal has been achieved, celebrate that achievement!

4. Is it normal to want to have time away from your spouse or alone time?

   Response: Yes, it is normal to enjoy some time to yourself to enjoy some of the things that you like to do as an individual. Sometimes, what one spouse enjoys, may not be what the other spouse enjoys. That is perfectly fine, because it allows you to have the time to relax and do something that you enjoy independently.

5. Why is communication so important in a marriage?

   Response: Communication is important because it is essential in any relationship. It helps to establish and articulate your needs, aspirations, desires, rules, and boundaries. In a marriage, it can be considered the "glue." Communication is the key to a marriage because it allows the marriage to function. Consider a computer: If you do not provide instructions to your computer, it will not function. Marriage has the same concept.

6. What do I do if my spouse does something that I can't stand and is one of my pet peeves?

    Response: You must express to your spouse that you have a problem with it and explain why you have a problem with it. If you express it, then your spouse will be able to understand it from your perspective.

7. What is the benefit of having good intimacy in a marriage?

    Response: It keeps both parties excited, and it keeps the fire burning.

8. What if my family does not like my spouse and speaks negatively about my spouse? What should I do?

    Response: The spouse with the family that is communicating negative comments, should talk with their family and inform them that you feel that it is hurtful when that occurs. It would be more acceptable for the spouse whose family is involved to communicate those thoughts. It helps to make the conversation a little easier.

9. What is your secret to making marriage last a lifetime?

    Response: For us, we are Christians, so our secret is to keep Jesus in it because it allows us to have a foundation with the principles of how to treat one another. We ensure that we first have a spiritual relationship with Jesus, then look to him for guidance on how to improve our physical relationship with each other. Also, we remember to enjoy "date night" with each other to allow it to continue to be a fun and exciting relationship.

10. What are some qualities that should never be in a marriage?

   Response: Unforgiveness, disrespect, unfaithfulness.

11. Why is it not a good idea to compare my marriage with someone else's?

   Response: It's not a good idea because everyone is unique. We all have had different life experiences that shape who we are. We all have different values, morals, and beliefs. You can't and shouldn't base your marriage experience on someone else's life.

12. Do you think people grow more in love each day?

   Response: We would like for people to grow more in love each day, but it depends on the relationship. Some people grow more bitter every day. Your relationship must be nurtured, by spending quality time together which allows you to grow together. You also want to experience fun activities, to help make the relationship more enjoyable. The fact of the matter is that it really depends on people going into the marriage with the right motives and intentions. Some people don't do that. But when they do, they are more willing to put forth the effort to nurture and cultivate with the right seeds in the marriage to allow each other to grow in love each day. You must put work into the relationship to allow yourselves to build that connection and bond, which would then allow you to begin to grow more in love each day.

13. Why is it so important to spend time together and continue to date even after you get married?

   Response: You want to keep building and nurturing the things that first caught your eye and made you so attractive to the other person. This is one of the seeds that can be sown in your marriage to allow you to continue to grow in love.

14. What should I do if my spouse likes to spend money and I like to save money?

   Response: You must sit down together and be willing to compromise. You must develop a plan where both of you can negotiate what works best for both of you. In this compromise, you should develop a budget, that includes how much money you both will save and spend. It's important to agree on a reasonable budget to attempt to make both spouses happy. Remember, no one wants to work, earn money, and still not be able to enjoy their money. So, agree on what you can both spend separately. Consider setting a certain financial limit that either one of you can't exceed without first discussing it with your spouse. You want to buy some of the things that you like and enjoy, but you also need to ensure that it fits well into your budget. The goal should be to live within your means.

15. What are some ways to handle conflict in a marriage?

   Response: First, understand that what works for one person may not work for another. One way to handle conflict is to talk about the conflict. However, sometimes you need to allow people time to "cool off" or calm down. It's difficult to get to a level of peace if you're highly upset. Then when you both are ready to have the discussion, identify the issue in the conflict so it's clear what the issue in question is. You both really need to understand what the conflict is and why it's a conflict. Both spouses need to articulate what the conflict is. Once the conflict has been identified, then you can explore ways to resolve the conflict and to see if there is a problem that's in your control. Consider if it is something that you can control, or if it's something out of your control. If it is a conflict that is in your control, see where you two can bend, and compromise on both sides. If it is something that is out of your control, then consider how you both can work to minimize the issue. That effective communication is extremely important because it is a valuable method to resolving conflict.

16. If my spouse has a lot of friends of the opposite sex, and that makes me uncomfortable, what should I do?

Response: First, explore the situation and ask yourself why you feel uncomfortable with your spouse's friends. Start with yourself first. Understanding why you are feeling insecure about the friendship is important. Is it something that you can control? Or is it the way your spouse interacts with their friends, or the way their friends interact with your spouse? If so, then talk with your spouse about your feelings. Generally, people don't mind friends of the opposite sex, but it's the things that you do with the friends or it's something about the friends that makes your spouse uncomfortable. So, have that discussion to understand the root cause of the feelings.

17. How important do you think self-care is?

Response: It is extremely important because how you take care of yourself influences how you take care of others. Self-care involves the mind, body, and spirit. If you don't take care of yourself, you won't have anything to pour out and give to others. It is important for your own mindfulness.

18. Why is it important to learn and understand my spouse's love language?

Response: You really want to satisfy your spouse so it can be a loving and meaningful experience. You want your spouse to feel fulfilled and ensure their needs are being met. It's important to communicate both of your love languages effectively to remove the guess work.

19. If I feel my spouse does not do a good job handling stress and anger, what should I do?

    Response: You should sit down and discuss it. Sometimes people aren't aware of how they handle stress and anger. So, you first ask them if they are aware of how they handle stress and anger and bring it to their attention. Then inform them how they handle stress and anger from your perspective and communicate to them how it makes you feel. That's where effective communication comes in. This type of behavior can affect a marriage negatively.

20. Do you think it is important for gender roles to exist in a marriage?

    Response: I don't think you need gender roles in a marriage. A couple should just do what they need to do to support their household. It is your choice what works best for you.

21. Is it important to share my life goals and expectations for the next 5-10 years?

    Response: Yes, you want to share your life goals and expectations that you have for your future. It's important so you both can know the direction in life that you desire to go in. It is important to establish your vision and goals so your spouse can help nurture them as well. If your spouse isn't aware of what those goals and ambitions are, then they can't help you work towards anything. Having goals and ambitions is a very attractive quality to have, and it helps your spouse feel secure about your future together.

www.ingramcontent.com/pod-product-compliance
Lightning Source LLC
Chambersburg PA
CBHW080835250626
47160CB00008B/2944